04.07.17

ILDFIRE

First published 2016 by Bloomsbury Education,
an imprint of Bloomsbury Publishing Plc
50 Bedford Square, London, WC1B 3DP

www.bloomsbury.com

Bloomsbury is a registered trademark of Bloomsbury Publishing Plc

A CIP catalogue for this book is available from the British Library

ISBN: 978-1-4729-1181-0

Printed in China by Leo Paper Products

1 3 5 7 9 10 8 6 4 2

recommended by

www.catchup.org

Catchup is a charity which aims to address the problem of underachievement
that has its roots in literacy and numeracy difficulties.

WILDFIRE

Sean Callery

Illustrated by Chris Askham

BLOOMSBURY EDUCATION
AN IMPRINT OF BLOOMSBURY

LONDON   OXFORD   NEW YORK   NEW DELHI   SYDNEY

CONTENTS

Chapter One

Loser

Sol's running feet pounded to the strong beat. The thumping music in his headphones blocked out the hum of his running machine. He smiled. He was running better than last time and he was breathing easily.

Maybe after a few more workouts he would be as fit as the tall boy in the cool tracksuit on the machine next to him.

The gold logo on the boy's expensive trainers flashed in the light. Sol tried to get a better look, but it was hard to see through the drops of sweat dripping from his untidy hair. He tapped the screen to stop his machine and reached for the towel that hung at the side. His wet hand slipped on the handle and grabbed at empty air. His feet kicked out and Sol tumbled to the floor.

"You twit," he laughed to himself. He could hear his voice over the music. He must have said it pretty loudly. Sol lifted the headphones from his ears and the busy sounds of the gym filled his head. Had he just shouted across the gym?

Bang. The boy on the next machine thumped the 'stop' button on his machine. Thud. His feet hit the floor and he leaned over Sol.

"What did you call me?" he snarled, his face inches away from Sol's.

"N... N... Nothing. I was talking to myself." Sol could just make out the boy's face through the sweat dripping into his eyes. "Sorry, Kyle."

He reached for his towel again but he slipped and his hand hit the wooden floor.

"No-one calls me names," said Kyle, stamping his foot on the towel. Keeping his eyes on Sol, he slowly wiped his trainers across it. "Especially losers like you." Kyle kicked the towel away and strode towards the heavy weights on the other side of the gym.

Sol tucked the dirty towel under his arm and pushed open the changing room door. The air was full of clothes – his clothes. Kyle's mates stopped throwing them around when the door creaked shut and Sol came in.

They sniggered as they pushed past him. "Tidy up, loser. You've made a mess," said Jaz as he shut the door. Sol could hear them laughing as they walked off down the corridor.

Sol dragged his tired feet past the benches and pegs to pick up his clothes. There was a sock missing. Kyle's gang always managed to lose something when they kicked his clothes around. He hoped that when he got through the survival trip, they would decide he wasn't a loser and would leave him alone.

Sol's face burned in the blast of hot air as he left the gym. He squeezed his eyes shut against the bright sun, pushed the headphones over his ears and blasted up the music. Thump. Thump.

It felt like the beat was his only friend.

Chapter Two

Meerkats

"Don't crunch those crisps so loud, I can't hear the telly," snapped Sol as his little brother sat down next to him on the bed.

"Sorry, Sol," said Fin.

"No, I'm sorry for shouting," said Sol, patting his brother's chubby knees and turning up the TV volume.

"These meerkats live underground in the cool earth, away from the scorching heat," said the TV guy.

"Will you sleep under the ground on your trip?" asked Fin.

"No, we'll be in a tent."

"You can have a midnight party like we did last summer," said his brother.

Sol wanted to say: "If I am in Kyle's group, his mates will have a party chucking my clothes in a ditch," but instead he said: "Maybe".

Fin laughed, as he did at almost everything Sol said.

On the TV show, the meerkats snarled and scratched at each other. "The leader tries to show he is the boss," said the commentary. Sol thought of Kyle. "But the challenger wins and now the pack has a new leader. The rest of the group works hard to please him," said the voice on the TV.

Sol thought of Kyle's mates. "Just like a gang of meerkats," he said.

"What?" said Fin, reaching for another bag of snacks.

"You shouldn't eat so many crisps," said Sol.

"Why not? You do," said Fin.

Now the meerkats were running. "The wind carries sparks so the fire travels really fast," said the TV voice. "These animals don't stand a chance."

"Have you got any more training to do?" asked Fin as he slurped on a fizzy drink.

"Shush, Fin," said Sol, his eyes on the screen as the meerkats ran away from the flames. "I have first aid training tomorrow."

Sol looked at the screen. The man was holding a box of matches and talking about how people can survive a fire that kills the animals.

"What is first aid?"

"How to keep people alive if they have an accident," said Sol, "Will you stop asking questions? I can't hear what he is saying."

"And that is how to fight fire with fire!" said the man, pointing to the flames zooming away up the hill behind him. "So remember, when faced with a problem, use STOP. The letters stand for Stop, Think, Observe, Plan. See you next time!"

"Why didn't he get burned?" asked Fin.

"I don't know," said Sol.

"But you know everything," said his little brother.

"You kept talking. I didn't see what he did," said Sol.

"What will the trip be like?" Fin asked.

Sol wanted to say: "It will be fine so long as I'm not in Kyle's group." But he didn't.

Instead, he said: "We get put into groups. We have to survive for two days in the wild, without any help. We feed ourselves and spend the night in our tents. No phone calls, and no hot drinks from Mum."

"Sounds scary," said Fin, sliding off the bed and heading for the door. "Mum, can I have a drink?" he yelled as he rushed down the stairs.

Sol stared at the TV screen. How had the TV guy survived the fire? It was as if the flames had gone right through him.

Chapter Three

Training

Sol felt like his chest was about to burst. Who would have thought that thumping a plastic dummy would be so tiring? He sank to the floor and enjoyed the cool feel of its wood on his skin.

"OK, that's enough," said the PE teacher, Miss Belper as she picked up her folder. "I think we've all got the idea of how to get the heart working again. At least, those of us who came to the training." She glanced at her list of names. Some had ticks next to them.

"They can't take the heat," said Kyle.

"None of us can take this heat for long," said Miss Belper. "Some boys came to the lessons about cooking and putting a tent up properly," she looked at her sheet. "But if they miss this first aid training they can't go on the trip."

Sol felt like he needed someone to thump his chest into life. There were only seven of them in the room, when there should have been ten to make two groups of five. If another one dropped out there might be only one group instead of two to do the trip. He'd be stuck with Kyle and his mates.

Miss Belper told them to have a drink. "You need water more than food. How long can you last without food? A day? A week?"

Sol remembered the TV programme he'd seen. "Ages, but without water you could die in three days."

"Very good, Sol. In this heat, you're going to need lots of water on your trip," said Miss Belper. "Right. So we've done the training on cooking and putting tents up and some basic first aid. Just to finish: what if someone breaks a leg or arm? Come here, Mikey." She picked up two big sticks and a bandage and showed everyone how to tie them round a broken limb to keep it straight.

"Mikey, work with Jaz. Kyle, come over here and work with Sol. We don't have to work with our best friends all the time, do we?" said Miss Belper

"Why do I have to work with him?" moaned Kyle.

"Sol hasn't been at our school long," said Miss Belper. She fixed her eyes on Kyle. "So we need to be kind to him."

Kyle grunted in protest. He left his friends and walked slowly towards Sol. He silently jammed the sticks on either side of Sol's arm and tied a bandage round to keep them in place.

Sol tried not to show it hurt as Kyle pulled the knot tight. Kyle turned away and walked back towards his friends.

"Go back please, Kyle," said Miss Belper.

"What for?" said Kyle

"He needs to practise on you. He might save your life one day!" said Miss Belper, smiling.

"I'd rather die," said Kyle, holding out his arm to Sol and staring at the door.

Chapter Four

One Group

"Look at the state of you!" laughed Sol.

Fin looked into the bedroom mirror and grinned. "I look like an alien!"

"A really hot, sweaty alien who has eaten a lot of chocolate," said Sol.

Fin pushed out his tongue to lick the dark, sticky mess. "It was all melted. There was no point putting it in your rucksack. I was just tidying up."

"Yeah, chocolate and heat don't mix," said Sol. He dropped the heavy rucksack on the floor. He had packed pasta, dried fruit and energy bars inside it along with his clothes and water bottles.

"Aren't you allowed any treats?" asked Fin, holding up a bag of crisps.

"If it stays as hot as this, even a drink of water will be a treat," said Sol.

"But you like these. Or you could trade them with your friends," said Fin, forcing the crisps into the side pocket of the rucksack.

Sol wished he did have friends to swap with. A couple of the quieter kids were OK, especially when they weren't with Kyle. Mikey smiled at him sometimes. He flicked on the TV.

"It is the hottest summer for thirty years," said a woman in the middle of a brown field. "Crops are dying. People are getting ill. And there is a high risk of wildfires."

"Why are the crops dying? Am I going to get ill? What's a wildfire?" asked Fin.

"Shush! I want to watch this!" snapped Sol.

"Why do you need these matches?" Fin said, waving the box in the air. "Oops," he said, as the contents spilled out. "Sorry. I only lost a few," he said, throwing the box into Sol's rucksack.

When Mum dropped him off at school next morning, Sol counted the rucksacks stacked against the minibus. Seven. Great. That was just enough to have two groups. He wouldn't have to go with Kyle and his mates.

"All aboard," called Miss Belper. "Are you alright, Mikey?" she called to a boy crouched in the middle of the car park.

"I feel dizzy," Mikey groaned.

"I think it must be the heat," said Mikey's dad, helping his son back into the car. "Sorry. I think he should stay at home after all."

Miss Belper knelt on the driver's seat, looking back into the minibus at the boys. "We need to look on the bright side. Maybe one big group is better than two smaller ones. There are more people to look after each other," she said, staring at Kyle. "And to take care of one another."

Two hours later, the group stood by a pile of rucksacks in the middle of a field.

"Does everyone have a phone for emergencies?" said Miss Belper. "You all came to the training on map-reading and staying safe. Good luck! I'll see you at the campsite this evening."

The minibus drove away. Sol could hear the buzz of insects. The six boys looked at each other. Kyle clapped his hands.

"Right, let's get out of this sun. Last one to that tree is a loser," said Kyle.

"First one there is the new leader," laughed Jaz. He kicked the others' rucksacks out of the way and ran off.

When Sol picked up his rucksack, there was a dark mark on the side.

He looked inside. Jaz's kick had broken one of his water bottles and split the plastic bag which had his phone inside. The phone lay in a puddle of water. He tried to unlock the wet phone. Nothing. His phone was dead.

Chapter Five

On the March

Sol walked to the steady beat of the music pounding through his headphones. He was glad that he did not use his phone to play music. And he was glad that the boys were too hot for much messing around. They walked in a line, following Kyle.

Sol was happy at the back and he was glad that the hours of training he had done gave him the strength to keep going. He reckoned he was doing better than some of the others.

The group flopped down in the shade of a tree and reached for their water bottles. Sol's was empty. Did he dare ask one of the others for a drink?

Jaz spat out a green lump of grass he had been chewing. Kyle flicked the map at a buzzing fly.

Flies. Sol remembered something from one of the TV programmes he had watched.

"Flies are never far from water," the TV guy had said. Stop, Think, Observe, Plan. Where would the water be? He looked downhill and spotted some bushes that seemed greener than the tired, brown plants nearby.

"Where are you going?" called Jaz, as Sol set off.

"I think there might be water over here," Sol called over his shoulder.

A minute later, Sol was pouring cool water over his head. He filled his spare bottle and returned to the group.

Jaz said, "I bet it has got loads of bugs in it."

Sol remembered something else from the programme. "Actually, most bugs have got fewer germs in them than that grass you chewed."

"Hey lads, we have an expert here!" said Jaz. "We should call you Survivor Boy. Come on, show Kyle where we are on the map. I reckon we're lost already."

"No we are not," said Kyle. "But I need to know which way is east."

"See for yourself," said Jaz, "Look out, everybody!" he called and he threw a compass towards Kyle. It hit Sol's head and bounced into the long grass.

"Ow!" exclaimed Sol.

"Don't lose it!" called Jaz. Sol jumped up to look for the compass.

Crunch.

Sol lifted his boot. The broken pieces of Jaz's compass glinted in the sun.

"You broke my compass!" cried Jaz. "How are we supposed to know which way is east now?"

Sol wanted to say that moss grows on the south side of trees, and they could work it out from that. But he didn't want to be called 'Survivor Boy' again.

"What a loser," said Kyle. "Anyhow, I think I know which way we need to go." Kyle set off, with the other boys behind him. Sol checked the green moss on the tree trunks as they walked on. Sure enough, there was way more on one side. That must be south. He looked at the direction Kyle was taking. They were going north, not east.

The row of boys in front of him made him think of the meerkats in the TV programme, following their leader. Sol knew Kyle was leading them the wrong way. He also knew that if he said anything, the others would just have another go at him. "At least I have learned something," he said to himself, "and that is that my feet hurt twice as much when they are going in the wrong direction.

Chapter Six

Split

Sol joined the other boys as they rested on the ground, drinking from their water bottles and panting for air. Kyle sat away from the others. He was staring at Jaz, who now held the map.

"I've got good news and bad news," said Jaz. "What do you want first?"

"Bad." They all chorused.

"The bad news is, we're going the wrong way. Survivor Boy over there broke the compass and that made us take the wrong path."

Five red faces glared at Sol.

"The good news is, I know how to get us out of this," said Jaz. He pointed to a high metal fence a few yards away. "I think we need to be on the other side of that fence. Our campsite is down in the valley. This path leads up a hill through the forest. If we climb that fence, we can go straight down towards the campsite."

"Are you sure?" said Kyle.

"Yep. Who is coming with me?" asked Jaz. The other boys stood next to him. Sol thought of the meerkats fighting to be leader.

Kyle pointed along the path they were on. "If we keep going along here we are sure to find a way down into the valley."

"Maybe," said Jaz, throwing his rucksack over the fence. "But it will take much longer. Come on lads!" He grabbed the mesh and pulled himself upwards. The fence shook and rattled until his feet thudded down on the other side.

Three of the boys looked at each other and, without a word, threw their rucksacks over the fence and then scrambled over themselves.

Sol remembered how easily the meerkats had accepted a new leader on the TV show. He looked up at the fence. He had got a lot fitter working out at the gym, but he knew his arms were weak and that fence was like a slippery cliff. Was he strong enough to climb it?

Kyle threw his bag over the fence, nearly hitting one of the other boys who was climbing over.

"Hey, watch out!" called the boy, falling down on the other side and swearing. "Look what you made me do!" he said, pointing at a huge rip in his trousers.

"No way am I risking that," said Kyle, "do you know how much these cost?" He pointed at the logo on his own trousers. "I reckon this way is quicker, anyway," he pointed along the path his side of the fence. "Chuck my rucksack back." Jaz picked it up and threw it high in the air.

"Cheers, losers," Kyle said as he caught it. "We are going to be at the campsite way before you – come on Sol."

Sol's mouth dropped open. Kyle had never used his proper name before. What should he do?

Jaz might be right about where they should be heading, but Sol didn't think he could climb the fence, and Miss Belper had told them that one of the golden rules of the trip was not to leave anyone on their own.

"We will be waiting for you. See you later, much later," laughed Jaz as he led the others down the hill.

Sol thought of the meerkats again as he fell into step next to Kyle. But Kyle took longer strides to keep himself ahead. "Stay behind me," he muttered, "I'm in charge."

Chapter Seven

The Fall

"You are going too fast," panted Sol.

"We need to get to that campsite before Jaz," muttered Kyle. "We need to get there first."

Sol wondered if Kyle was talking to himself or to him.

It was cooler in the shade of the tall, green trees. Kyle began taking even longer steps. Sol stumbled to a stop and reached for his water bottle. A gust of wind cooled his hot cheeks.

Could he smell smoke? He heard a faint shout. Tiny in the distance, Kyle pointed and shouted, "This way. Follow me."

Sol raised a thumb to show he had heard, even though Kyle had already raced off. When he reached the turning, Sol found a path leading down to the valley. Where was the campsite? He strained his eyes to look for the colourful tents. He saw a flash of orange a long way down behind the trees.

It was harder walking downhill and Sol's knees hurt. His heavy boots dragged on the ground and the sweat dripping into his eyes made everything seem blurred like a bad picture. In the sudden bright light of a clearing he saw a thick tree root across the path just in time to lift his heavy feet over it. Then he almost stumbled into a log.

A strange log. It was blue. Sol blinked the sweat away and looked again. Kyle lay across the path and his foot was twisted at a funny angle.

"Kyle, are you OK?" he asked.

Kyle's face was pale and his eyes were closed.

Chapter Eight

Fire

Sol tried to remember the checks from the first aid lesson. He looked around – there was no sign of danger nearby, like broken glass or a snake. Kyle must have tripped on the tree root that had nearly caught out Sol.

He pushed Kyle's mouth open. Nothing there to choke Kyle and he could hear the faint sounds of the boy breathing in and out. When he rested his hand on Kyle's neck to feel for the pulse, the boy's eyes suddenly opened.

"Get off me!" yelled Kyle.

"OK. OK. Take it easy, Kyle," said Sol.

"Got to get there first," said Kyle. He tried to stand up but fell back. "Ow! My ankle!"

Sol looked at how Kyle's foot lay at an odd angle and said, "I think it might be broken."

"It hurts." Kyle hardly moved his mouth as he spoke. "I can't get up."

"We need to stop it moving," said Sol, looking around for some straight sticks like the ones Miss Belper had used.

It felt good to have something to do. Ten minutes later, a tight bandage covered sticks that held Kyle's floppy ankle in place.

"You still can't walk on it," warned Sol.

"I know," said Kyle. "I feel dizzy and I can smell smoke. It must be the pain."

"Have a drink," said Sol, reaching for his bottle. He sniffed. There it was again: the smell of smoke. Where was it coming from? Maybe it was the campsite. He looked down the valley to where he had seen the flash of the orange tent.

He saw orange all right, but it was moving. And above it there were wisps of smoke.

The orange wasn't a tent. It was flames. The forest was on fire.

Kyle saw it too. "Wildfire!" he cried. "This is an emergency. Phone for help."

"My phone is bust," said Sol. "Where is yours?"

Kyle checked his bag and swore. "It was in the pocket. It must have fallen out when Jaz threw it over the fence," he said. "But that fire won't get to us before they send help, will it?"

Sol thought about the TV programme he had seen. "Fire travels up hills faster than down them," the reporter had said. "And evergreen trees burn much faster than trees that lose their leaves."

He looked at the layer of pine needles in the clearing. The trees all around them were evergreens. The fire would burn them fast. He took a deep breath. What had the TV guy said to do in an emergency?

Stop. Well, they had no choice about that.

Think. He was trying!

Observe. He could do more than see the fire. Now he could hear it crackling.

Plan. That was where he got stuck. Kyle could not move. Even if Sol left him and ran off, the fire would catch him up.

They were going to burn.

Chapter Nine

Plan

The TV guy had said: "And that is how to fight fire with fire!" Sol closed his eyes and tried to re-run the programme in his head.

"What are you doing?" asked Kyle, as Sol grabbed his rucksack and pulled out his blanket.

"You have to trust me. I have a plan," said Sol, as he rolled Kyle onto the blanket and pulled it to the edge of the clearing.

"What plan?"

"I saw it on TV," said Sol. He kicked piles of pine needles into the middle of the clearing and reached into his bag for the matches. There were only a few left. Strike. As the flames rose from the match he pushed it into the pile of needles. A wisp of smoke rose. Then it disappeared.

He fumbled for another match and tried again. A bigger wisp of smoke, then nothing.

Sol shook the box of matches.

There was only one left. He didn't dare try the same method again – he only had one chance now.

The crackle of the flames coming towards them reminded him of his brother crunching crisps while they had watched the TV programme. If only Fin hadn't done that – Sol probably missed a vital tip on how to start a fire.

Of course.

Crisps.

He remembered a science lesson where the whole class cheered as the teacher gave out crisps and told the class to set fire to them. The snacks had burned amazingly well.

He dug in his bag and pulled out the packet of crisps.

"Oh great! Time for a snack is it?" yelled Kyle.

Sol emptied the crisps into a small pile and struck the last match. As soon as it reached the crisps, little yellow flames flickered. He added a few pine needles, then more, waiting each time for them to flare up. After a few minutes, the flames started to sizzle and burn more pine needles and the fire spread across the clearing.

"You are going to kill us both!" said Kyle as Sol pulled the blanket from under him. Sol tipped the bottle of water over the blanket, then leapt across the flames and started to damp down the fire from the middle outwards.

He could feel the heat through the soles of his boots, and the smoke made him choke, but after a few minutes he was standing inside a large circle of charred ground.

"No!" cried Sol, as he saw Kyle trying to crawl towards the bushes. "Those will be on fire in a minute!"

Kyle groaned as Sol rolled him back into the middle of the clearing. Soot gathered like black snot stains under their noses.

Sol grabbed a fresh shirt from his bag, ripped off both sleeves and poured the last of the water over them.

"Hold this over your face," he said. "It will help you breathe."

"What happens now?" asked Kyle, his face suddenly yellow from the light of the flames in the trees around them.

"We wait," said Sol.

"Wait to die?"

"We let the fire pass. It can't set fire to the ground that is already burnt."

"Are you sure about this?"

"Yes," Sol said. He crossed his fingers behind his back.

Chapter Ten

Blaze

The smoke felt like grit in Sol's throat and made his nose itch and his eyes water. He heard Kyle coughing. Sol could see the fire reflected in Kyle's eyes as he watched the blaze racing towards them.

"It is alright for you," croaked Kyle. "You can run."

"I can," agreed Sol. "But I won't."

His face felt tight, as if someone was tugging at the skin. He pushed the wet cloth against his nose and tried not to cough.

The needles of the nearest tree fizzed like a million firecrackers and the long, branches rattled as they clattered and snapped against each other. The sizzle and crackle of the fire became a roar like thunder. The tree's blackened trunk exploded, sending up a fountain of sparks.

A shower of orange embers rained down on them. The boys flicked at them as if they were in a swarm of blazing flies.

Suddenly, Sol noticed a spark on Kyle's arm. He pointed and shouted "YOUR SLEEVE IS BURNING!" but he could hardly hear his own voice over the roar of the fire.

He sprang across and bashed Kyle's arm, feeling pin-pricks of heat from the sparks. When he lifted his hand, there was a small, black-rimmed hole in sleeve. Then there was a thud on his skull, and another. Through the clouds of smoke he saw Kyle's hands flying towards his head again and again.

Was Kyle punching him as a punishment for bashing him? Didn't he know Sol had stopped his clothes from catching fire? Kyle's mouth was opening and closing and Sol made out some of the words "HAIR... FIRE... YOUR..."

Sol slid his hands over his head, feeling tiny bursts of heat from the sparks that had settled in his hair. Finally, Kyle gave him the thumbs up.

A few metres away, Sol's rucksack sank slowly into the ground. It looked as if it was falling into a hole. Sol gasped when he saw the plastic cover change shape as it melted in the fierce heat. But he had heard his own gasp. That was good. That meant the roar of the fire was getting quieter. Slowly, it became a gentle sizzle and the crashing of falling branches became more distant. Sol twisted his neck to peer through the clouds of smoke. The whole clearing and the trees around it was charred black, and grey smoke rose in plumes around them.

The two boys lay on their backs and stared at the widening patch of blue sky above them. Sparks danced across it like crazed butterflies. Kyle turned his ash-grey face to Sol and said "Fancy a barbecue, mate? I think this arm is cooked!"

They laughed, and then choked as the smoke crept into their hot, dry throats.

Chapter Eleven

Choice

Sol's running feet pounded to the strong beat. The thumping music in his headphones blocked out the hum of his running machine. He smiled. He was going way faster than the tall figure on the machine next to him.

A big drop of sweat hung from the untidy hair over his eyes. He tapped the screen to slow the machine speed and reached for his towel. But his legs had turned to jelly and he grabbed thin air as his feet kicked out and he tumbled to the floor.

The boy on the next machine bashed the 'stop' button, jumped off the machine and leaned over Sol. "You twit!" laughed Kyle, throwing the towel in his face, "You look like you're melting!"

While Sol wiped himself down, Kyle said, "Me and the lads are going to see a film tonight. Do you want to come?"

"Maybe," said Sol. "I'll text you. See you later," he said, and headed for the door. When he reached the changing room, he had to step over the clothes scattered across the floor. But his were hanging from a peg, just as he had left them. Jaz and the gang ran out of the showers, flicking their towels at each other.

"You've made a mess," said Sol.

"Nah, it wasn't us," said Jaz. "Are you coming to see the film tonight?"

"Maybe," said Sol.

"We need you there, mate," said Jaz, "in case the cinema burns down!"

Sol's face burned in the blast of hot air as he walked outside. He squeezed his eyes shut against the bright sun, pushed the headphones into his ears and blasted up the music. Thump. Thump.

He felt as strong as the beat.

Fin sat on Sol's bed, flicking through a comic.

"What are you doing tonight?" he asked through a mouthful of crisps.

"The lads want me to go and see a film," said Sol.

"Cool," said Fin.

"But actually, little brother, I could do that another time." Sol switched on the TV.

"There's a show about how to survive at the North Pole. I thought we could take a look."

"Maybe you will get to go on a trip there," said Fin.

"Yeah, maybe I will," said Sol. "But I'm not letting you help pack my bag this time. That way I will have enough matches."

"OK," said Fin, throwing his empty crisp packet and missing the bin. "You will know how to survive."

"Yes," grinned Sol. "I do."

Bonus Bits!
Feelings and Emotions

This story makes us think about how people treat one another.

Why do you think Kyle and his friends targeted Sol in the way they did?

Do you think they were right to do this?

How do you think Sol felt when Kyle wiped his foot on his towel?

How do you think Sol felt when he saw his clothes all over the changing room floor?

Do you think Kyle's gang are like a group of meerkats?

Do you think Sol is looking forward to the trip?

Why did Sol think Kyle was hitting him in the head? What made him think this as his first thought?

How do you think Sol felt at the end when he saw someone else's clothes thrown around the floor?

Wildfires

Can you really fight fire with fire like Sol does in the story? Yes! In Australia they sometimes do this to control the huge wildfires they have when the weather is hot and dry.

By burning a strip of forest they can stop the fire spreading further. It can protect farm animals, people and buildings. The controlled fire uses up the things a fire needs to spread.

This is only ever done by people who know what they are doing as if the fire gets out of control, things could get even worse than they were to start with!

Who said what?

Read each quote below and decide which of these characters said it:

1. Fin
2. Mikey
3. Jas
4. Kyle
5. Sol
6. TV commentator
7. Miss Belper

Check back in the book to if you need to.

A "Stay behind me, I'm in charge."

B "Tidy up loser. You've made a mess."

C "I look like an alien!"

D "Just like a gang of meerkats."

E "And that is how to fight fire with fire."

F "Sol hasn't been at our school long."

G "I feel dizzy."

What next?

What might have happened if the boys had gone on their trip in the winter? Why not plan and write a story set in winter instead? Think about what the weather might be like and how they could stay warm.

Answers to "Who said what?"

A: 4 (Kyle)

B: 3 (Jas)

C: 1 (Fin)

D: 5 (Sol)

E: 6 (TV commentator)

F: 7 (Miss Belper)

G: 2 (Mikey)

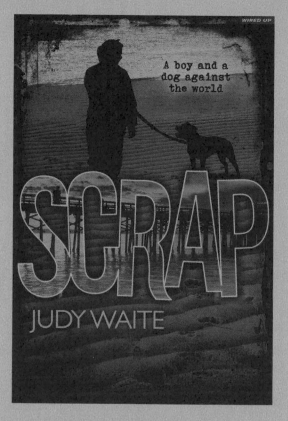

A boy and a dog against the world

WIRED UP

SCRAP

JUDY WAITE

9781472909381

Lewis hates the gangs that hang out on the beach. When he finds a stray dog tied to the pier he knows it was the gangs. Can he help her before the tide comes in?

NEW!

9781472910172

Nic takes his friends to a Halloween party to try to impress them, but soon things take a frightening turn.

Welcome to a party unlike any other...